The Inheritance Mysteries

Wine & Lies

Book 1

Author's Note

This story is a work of fiction. Any places, events or characters mentioned are products of the author's imagination or used fictitiously. Any similarity to real events, characters or places is unintentional.

This book, either in its entirety or in part may not be reproduced or distributed in any form without written permission from the author. That includes 'modelling'.

Front cover photo thanks to Ylanite Koppens from Pexels

Chapters

Introduction

It all began one rainy day in Surry, England. At the time I had no idea what was beginning, or where it would end up. What I thought was the start, and subsequent end, proved only to be the tip of the proverbial iceberg.

I am Georgina, Wakefield, five foot six inches tall, have shoulder length, wavy red hair, a good figure, thanks to nature, not diet, and am generally considered pretty. I am thirty-one and have worked in the wine industry since leaving school.

Until recently I believed my grandparents on my father's side were dead. When I discovered my grandfather was still living, I tried to contact him, but with no success. He returned my letters, unopened, and refused my calls. For that reason, I was astonished to find he had left me his estate.

This comprised a Château in France, along with a thriving wine business. It also included a built-in family living there, who hated me with a passion, even though we had never met, and a secret that could get me into a whole lot of trouble if it ever became known.

Philip, the lawyer handling the will, foresaw many problems for me right from the beginning. He explained that he had a range of sealed enveloped he was to use in a variety of situations, so if anything happened, I was to contact him.

If you have read another story in the Inheritance Mysteries series you can skip the first four pages of the prelude, as this explains how this series of books came into existence, and you already know that story.

Only the last pages are different, as they explain a little more about this particular story.

Prelude

Let us introduce ourselves before we begin and explain our connection to Georgina. I am Henry Witherspoon, this is Philip Thompson, over there is Stephen Sumner. We are all lawyers who met at university. We also share a common hobby, mystery books and stories.
At university the three of us started a club for like-minded people, where we would take existing cold cases and examine them, using the precious information in the university library. We also took advantage of the university's valuable connections, which allowed us access to such evidence as the police had available. This included their files and notes.

The first case we looked at, we didn't do a particularly good job of, but the second one we actually solved. Something the police had failed to do. Between the three of us we found what we thought were vital clues that had been overlooked, then we took them to their logical conclusion. Once we had all our findings we spoke to our professor at the university, who, after he had looked at the material, and agreed with us, accompanied us to the police station. The police force may not have listened to us had we gone alone, although they did listen to the Professor. It was actually our information that helped solve the case. This made us popular with some policemen; those who genuinely wanted to help the public, but it also made us unpopular with other policeman. Ones who didn't like being shown up and wanted the credit for having solved the case themselves. Their vanity, along with a promotion, were more important to them than helping the victims.

After that we became famous on campus, therefore many other students, who had been reluctant before, now wished to join our club, and we were inundated with membership requests. We whittled these down to a total of ten members, choosing the ones we believed were closest to our way of thinking, as we were sure too many would confuse issues, rather than solving them.

Our little club investigated many more cases, even solving a few of them, but nowhere near the number we would have liked. Still, we did better than the experts had done. Plus, we had loads of fun along the way.

Once we graduated, we all got jobs in different sectors, such as civil, criminal, and industrial law, but the three of us founding members kept in touch as well as keeping up a crime solving club.

One day I drew up a will for someone. The heirs came back to me a few months later to complain that there were all sorts of complications with their inheritance. Dear only knows what they expected me to do. Even when I pointed out that all I had done was follow my client's wishes, they still expected some sort of miracle from me.

If they did not want to run the business together, they were not obliged to. The will only stated that if they wanted to inherit the multimillion-dollar company, they had to run it successfully for five years, and they must all work collectively the entire time. After that, they could sell it, keep it, put in a manager, or do whatever they wanted with it. It was theirs, free and clear at that point.

If they didn't want to work as a unit, the business, a very successful human resource's agency, would go to someone else. What is more, I was not allowed to disclose who that would be, but it was the current manager, who had no idea that he might be in line for a multimillion-dollar gift.

The heirs wanted the business, weren't prepared to lose it, however they weren't prepared to work together. The result was a host of visits from each of them in turn, complaining about something, and that was where my idea for our current business came from.

The greedy offspring found mystery where there was none, failing to look at the only unknown fact – why their uncle, who had barely known them, made the stipulation they all had to work together. (I investigated that on my own time, finding out he was a sadistic type of man who enjoyed creating difficulties – hence the codicil in his will.)

That started the train of thought that brings us to where we are today.

I spoke to my friends, who both loved my idea, therefore for a few years we each worked as hard as we could to earn enough money to fund our venture. We also undertook as much will writing as the companies we worked for would let us do. We wanted practice in this field, to see what people left, how they left it, and how the heirs managed things afterwards.

Initially our idea of the heirs writing an account of 'what happened next', was simply to satisfy our own curiosity, but once we had a couple of stories, which were quite unique, as well as totally thrilling, Philip had casually said it would make a marvellous book. It was out of that utterance, the rest of the idea came.

Once we were ready, we all gave in our notice at our various jobs, and started her own firm, 'Will The Future'. Initially the clients who came to us did not want to add a caveat to their will stating their heirs must sign a contract agreeing to write notes on how they progressed after inheriting whatever it was. However, we had anticipated this, which was why we had worked so hard to get so much money. Our healthy bank balance meant we could afford to turn people away and refuse work if this part was not met. We waited until clients did accept it.

Our first client to agree to our terms was an elderly gentleman of the old school. He belonged to a gentlemen's club and thought the whole thing 'a hoot', his words not ours. For this reason, he talked endlessly about our clause in his club. This promoted a great deal of interest, with many of his friends believing it sounded fun too. Word spread, meaning business grew.
As if to help our venture, Philip had married an editor for a publishing company, (he genuinely fell in love with her, the coincidence was just pure luck). That guaranteed our books were at least read, the first step to putting out a book, then the publisher, once we handed them over, liked them too, which was the second part.

One of the books that we published became a bestseller, (third, and last part to a having a successful book career), then it was picked up for a film, (an unexpected bonus). That was when things really took off.

Once clients knew that their life story in some way could become a Hollywood movie, everybody wanted us. Our business became very successful, earning a large amount of money from our books, so were able to charge a very low fee for doing the wills. This made it accessible to people who perhaps didn't have enough money to pay large lawyer's fees. Our only criteria for accepting someone was that there had to be something that indicated the possibility of mystery, and of course they must agree to put our caveat in their will as well.

As business progressed, we needed to hire a couple more lawyers to deal with the work. It took some time to find ones who were able to judge what may or may not have a mystery surrounding it, but eventually we built up a decent team and things took off. Soon Philip's wife left the job she was in to start her own publishing company. Obviously, she had an exclusive contract for all our books.

One day a man entered our offices looking very dapper, if you did not count the fact that he didn't suit his clothes. You could say he was well dressed, but he looked as if he was better suited to a workingman's clothes. A 'thug in sheep's clothes' was how one of us dubbed him, and that best explains what we all saw.

With an English accent, he said his name was the Comte de Chivagnon. He told us he owned the Château de Chivagnon where they made a very prestigious wine. Once he gave us the name of the wine, *Allisette*, we did recognise it, for it was considered to be among the best of wines.

He spun us a lot of tales, which at the time we had no reason, except instinct, to doubt. Later, when we started to do some research, we found it was all, or at least mostly, a load of nonsense.

We had to ask for documents as proof of identity in order to properly draw up his will, and it was here his stories started to unravel. The first time he came to us, he said he had no identity documents with him but would return. We didn't see him for over a year. This alone intrigued us.

When he returned, without explaining the long lapse of time, he presented his documents. It turned out his name was Bert Wakefield, and he was British by birth. He had invented his title, or rather when he married the Comte de Chivagnon's daughter, he took over her father's title when that noble man died, there being no heirs. Again, this wasn't strictly true, as unaware of his good fortune, there was one heir, wandering somewhere in the depths of Australia or New Zealand. What had happened, was with no one to challenge him taking the title, Bert had appropriated it and used it uncontested.

He was on his fourth wife, (if you did not count the two annulments he had paid generously to get). He had been married to his current wife for six years at that time, and she, along with her three grown-up children, lived at the Château. The children worked in the winery, and the wife was chatelaine of the Château, running the castle to rigid rules. Since his first wife had died, this wife also appropriated the title of Comtesse.

Amazingly, perhaps, all these lies and deceit were actually not the thing that intrigued us, that was something else.

He was leaving everything to a granddaughter who he had never seen. He merely knew of her existence. He specifically wanted included in the will that his current wife, and her children, were to get nothing from him. If or when they left the Château it was to be with only the clothes they were wearing. His granddaughter was not to give them anything at all. This part fascinated us. He intended to continue living with his wife and her children, so why shut them out of any inheritance?

We tried to point out that by French law, family were entitled to at least half of everything, so legally he could not exclude his wife. He insisted it must be done his way and we were not to worry about the rest. To this end he left us another envelope, which we were to open and use if his wife, or any of her children, contested the will. It was all quite intriguing. He assured us inside it was enough to stop her taking his home and business. When we expressed doubts about this, fearing blackmail, he assured us it was nothing of the sort, again repeating we were not to worry.

If his granddaughter ran the winery successfully for two years, she was to receive a sealed letter he entrusted to our care. His friend, Jacques Durand, would judge if the winery was successful or not. We also got a set of sealed instructions, two actually; one if his granddaughter achieved the goal he set and made a success of the winery, thereby receiving one envelope, and the other if she didn't. All of these were only to be opened if the conditions he specified were met. That meant there was at least one envelope, the contents of which we would never know; depending on whether she was successful or not. This too fascinated us, at the same time as driving us mad that we would never know the contents. (Opening it before shredding, was unethical, however tempting it may be.)

Chapter 1

"Georgina, come in and sit down for a minute. We need to talk to you," my parents said, in what I felt was an ominous tone. I entered, gingerly, sure from their tone I was about to hear something I wasn't going to like.

They both hemmed and hawed a lot, then decided we all needed a drink before they gave me the news. My stomach dropped. Were they going to get divorced? Is that what it was? Was one of them ill? That would be worse than them splitting up.

I sat feeling sick until we all had drinks, then I said, "Please tell me. It sounds like you have something horrible to say, but I need to know."

"It's not necessarily horrible dear," my mother said, with a failed attempt at a smile. "It's just something we have never told you. We might even have lied to you about it in a fashion."

My father took over at this point. "You know we always told you my parents, your grandparents, were dead, well that's not quite true. Your grandmother is dead, but your grandfather isn't.
He disowned me when I didn't want to work in the family business and, in his words, disavowed me as well. I tried to contact him a few times, but my letters were returned unopened. I even sent him pictures of you to let him know he had a grandchild, but still no response, so I gave up. He's not dead, but he might as well be."

This didn't seem that big a deal. Okay, so they had lied, he wasn't dead, but in another sense he was, because he didn't exist in my life. Unless he had asked to see me. Maybe that was why they were telling me this now, I reasoned.
Before jumping to any conclusions, I asked that simple question.

I wasn't sure if they were ignoring my question or getting to it in a roundabout way, but my father answered, "The thing is, now that you are going to France to do that sommelier course, there is a chance you will come across him. He lives in France, and is in the wine business. You know his wine, you even like it. He makes Allisette wine, as well as bottling the Mexican wine, Mondez."

"We didn't want you to run into him accidentally and not know," my mother added.

There were a few things that weren't adding up. I knew that Allisette wine was made by the Comte de Chivagnon. Did that mean he was my grandfather? Was my father French nobility as well? That question had to be asked straight away.
The answer apparently was no, because 'Comte' was only a title my grandfather used, but had no legal right to do so. He was English but had married a French noblewoman and got his hands on her father's estate.
My father loosened up at that point, enough to give me more information. "He was never a particularly nice man, and in some ways it was that, as much as anything, that made me not want to work there. As you know, I'm also not that interested in wine, unlike you. Then I met your mother, and we decided to start the publishing business

together. That was such a success that it took up all our time. I've never regretted my choice, nor missed the tyrant who was my father. He is now a considerable age, but is still running the winery, along with his sixth wife and her three children. A younger version of a blonde bimbo each time, naturally.

"Why now? Why didn't you ever tell me? All the times I was studying wine and talked about Allisette wine, you could have said something. When I brought bottles of it home, you could have told me the picture of the château on the label was the house where you grew up."

"Darling," my mother said, "when you were a baby you were too young to understand. We didn't want you hurt by the knowledge that he didn't want to see you. By the time you were old enough to understand, it just seemed easier to keep things going the way they were. There was no reason to tell you, as you would have gained nothing from the information. By then, it had reached a point when it seemed too late to say anything. Please forgive us. We didn't do it to harm you, but to protect you, and then I guess we kept doing it to protect ourselves. If we told you, we had to admit to lying to you. We didn't want you to hate us, or be angry with us for having lied to you." My mother looked close to tears as she finished that spiel. Although I knew they had lied to me, I didn't like seeing her like that, I could see why they had done it in the beginning, and why they felt it was too late once I was old enough to fully understand.

I went to my mother and hugged her. 'I don't like the fact that you lied to me, but I do understand, and appreciate that it started for my own sake. I can also see that it then felt too late to change the story. But I still don't understand why you're telling me now. I know what you said about me going to France, but his winery is a long way from Paris., So the chances of me running into him are virtually nil. Also, from everything you have said, it is not as if he is going to try to contact me. So why?" I heard some of the desperation I was feeling in my voice.

I was terribly confused. I was angry and disappointed that they had lied to me, but I loved them dearly. They had done so much for me all my life; taking me to tennis when I wanted, music lessons and paying for any wine course I showed an interest in. I desperately wanted to understand, so I could forgive them.

It was my father who replied. "There is a very senior man in the Union des Sommeliers, where you are going, who will probably remember your grandfather from back when he was Bert Wakefield. There is a chance he will recognise your surname and ask if there is any connection. He may not, but it is a chance we didn't want to take. We felt, bad as it is, that you needed to hear it from us." He seemed to be done by then as silence followed, although there was something in his expression that made me think he wanted to say more.

"What is it? There's more. Something you're not telling me."

"You might be better to pretend you're not a relation of Bert Wakefield's. He cheated, lied and conned everyone he met, so anyone who does remember him, will feel very bitter towards him. He cost more than one person their family heritage. Gustave Boule, the man in the Union des Sommeliers, lost his vineyard, along with his home. It had been in his family for centauries and his son committed suicide, feeling responsible. It was him that my father conned out of everything you see. I wouldn't want him, or any of the others to take their revenge out on you. As I said, he may have been my father, but he was not a nice man."

I sat for a while thinking, having returned to my chair after hugging my mother. This was a lot to take in, not least that my father was suggesting I perpetuate the lie by saying I was not related to Bert.

"You could always say you are not aware of any relations in France, or your parents told you your grandfather was dead, and blame us," my mother suggested.

"I'm going to take Mulberry for a walk. I need some time to get things clear in my head." I stood up, and donning my jacket called for our cocker spaniel who was always happy to oblige, if he got to walk out of it.

He and I headed through the fields behind our house going towards the wood. He ran around having fun, enjoying chasing the sticks I threw for him until we came to the river. There I sat on a stone, and he sat down beside me. Somehow stroking his head help me feel calmer, more able to put things into some sort of perspective.

Chapter 2

I have no idea how long I spent sitting by the flowing water, but eventually Mulberry let me know he had had enough and wanted to go back.

I had come to terms with my parent's deceit, but was still unsure what to do about my grandfather.

I had worked too long and too hard to get where I was for a man I had never met to ruin everything. It appeared the only sure way I had to stop that happening, was to pretend no connection. It was only as we were crossing the field behind the house that the solution came to me. 'I have no grandfather' was all I had to say. That was true, for I didn't, not in the way that counted anyway. He was not a part of my life. Let anyone who asked, make whatever they wanted of that phrase; they could believe he was dead, or they could believe I wanted nothing to do with him. Either way it should satisfy any desire for revenge whoever faced me might have, without compromising my future.

As I reached out to open the back door it suddenly came to me; that is exactly what my parents had done with me. They had taken the easiest road, that which worked out best for them. The only difference was, they also believed it was best for me, and now armed with the knowledge of this man, I couldn't but agree. I realised that I had had to know, in case the subject came up while I was in Paris, but I had been better off not knowing he was alive.

It was only later, while I was in France, that I decided to write to him. At that point I had heard a lot about the ogre, nothing ever good. Nevertheless, he was my grandfather, and I thought I would like to meet him. This feeling was something I couldn't explain even to myself, curiosity perhaps. As I said, I don't really know what prompted this idea, but it was there nonetheless.

Just as my parents had said, he didn't want to meet me. My letter was returned unopened, and nothing could have been a clearer signal than that. Trying once I could justify to myself, but I would not try again.

Lessons progressed, and as one of the most important wines, Allisette was often talked about. Our teachers believed that background knowledge of the wineries was just as important as the wine they produced, so I learnt a lot about the way Château de Chivagnon produced its wines and how the Comte de Chivagnon had built up his empire.

There was nothing illegal about anything he had done, at least nothing anyone could find. Many had tried, and the list of official investigations into the Comte's conduct was very long, but always resulted in a lack of proof. One recent example of this was when a competitor of Allisette wine had their crops accidentally sprayed with weed killer. The pilot responsible explained he had been paid to spray weedkiller anonymously, over the telephone, but he had no reason to doubt the authenticity of the call. He was certain the voice on the end of the line was a woman's, and it was this more than anything, that let the count off the hook. Not only was the winery's entire crop destroyed, but the land was so contaminated it couldn't be replanted for a couple of years. This would have ruined Monsieur Moreau, had it not been for a group of vintners who each made a small investment in his winery, allowing him to keep the land and his home. It also permitted him to replant once the land stopped being toxic. His first yield would be a small one because the funds were only sufficient to replant one of the many fields he used. It would be enough to get back into business, provided that is, the same thing did not happen again. The Moreau family had been there for generations and their wine had been as good as, if not better than, Allisette, so it was considered sacrilege to have ruined such a historical crop and a respected dynasty.

I couldn't believe nothing could be found against the count. For seven of his competitors to suffer disasters, never the same one twice, but bringing total ruin each time, seemed to go way beyond coincidence. When I mentioned this in class, I was told that the law needed proof, and besides it was made to protect people, not land or fruit. Even in France, where wine was an age-old tradition, the law appeared not to have been updated since it was first made. This allowed the count to carry on making his wine with more success each year as his competitors suffered assorted ill fortune.

It has to be said, from that point on I joined the ranks of people wanting to make him pay. If I came across two wines that were more or less equal, I deliberately did not recommend his wine. When I wrote reviews, I came down hard on anything negative I found in his wine, rather than focusing on anything positive. Unfortunately for me, his wine was excellent, of consistently high quality, and that made it hard to criticise it too much. I would ruin my own good name if I went too far, but I felt I had to do whatever I could to downplay his wine and let others have the chance he did his best to deny them.

I had always wanted to be a sommelier, and even as a child my father had commended me on my palette. He had started me tasting wines when I was about twelve, explaining notes, tones and anything else I needed to know in order to distinguish one wine from another. I had fallen in love with wine, so a choice of career had been an easy decision.

While there are a couple of vineyards in Britain, they aren't really anything worth mentioning. As far as I was concerned, actually nearly everybody in the industry agreed with me, French wine was still the best. That was what was taking me to France, to the (UdS), *Union des Sommeliers* in Paris. I was going to do a course and hopefully be certified by them as a Maître Sommelier, which is the top title in the wine field. It is also one seldom awarded.

Everything I had done since I left school had been geared towards reaching this level, and if I got the certificate, I could choose just about any job I wanted, (in the wine industry obviously). I hadn't actually decided on my final job, but at one point, a top auction house had invited me to be their wine consultant. I had accepted on a temporary, freelance basis, and loved it. They dealt in all sorts of antiquities and art. I enjoyed seeing these beautiful objects, spending any spare time I had there listening to the experts give their opinion on their provenance, history and value. The only downside to that job was I had to value wine without opening it, so I didn't get to taste anything. I knew from experience, that was not the type of job for me.

A couple of top restaurants had approached me as well, asking me to be their head sommelier. There I would have had a chance to taste many different wines, but that seemed somewhat boring and limiting. Once I knew what a certain bottle tasted like, it was simply a question of making sure the others from the same vineyard hadn't gone off. This was probably the best paying of all jobs, however it was the one that interested me the least. No, that's not strictly true. Another avenue I could have gone down was to teach, and that definitely was the one that interested me the least.

Had finances allowed I would have opened a wine shop. I knew what I wanted to sell, a full price range of only quality wine. I knew that most people didn't have the money or knowledge to appreciate an expensive bottle, so I would need to stock cheaper wines as well. This didn't worry me, because there were some good, reasonably priced wines, especially from South Africa. I would have a few bottles open to let people have a little taste, so they knew what they were getting. That way they would be happy with their purchase, and it would take the risk factor out of it. Many of my friends complained about this when they bought a bottle of wine, explaining that unless they stuck to the same one they knew, it was always a chance because they may or may not like a different one. However, to open such a shop, with stock, would cost a fortune, and that was a fortune neither I nor my family had.

I intended to get my certificate, if I could, and then decide. I always had the auction house job to keep me going until I made a final choice.

I had never really stopped living at home for a very good reason; I was either studying or working in a different place every year. I would find somewhere furnished to rent in whatever area I was in, then when that job ended, go back home until the next one. There was no point in buying my own house until I knew where I needed to buy it. I had earned a reasonable amount in all the jobs I had done so far, and certainly had enough for a deposit, if not to pay entirely for a house, providing was small.

Chapter 3

I was two days away from getting my certificate when it happened. I had already been told by the UdS that they loved my work and I would be certified as a Maître Sommelier at the award ceremony.
I was called into the head's office where a serious looking man with a briefcase was waiting for me.
When we were left alone, he identified himself as Philip Thompson, lawyer for the Comte de Chivagnon. He regretted to inform me my grandfather had passed away, but was delighted to inform me that he would like me to visit their office to discuss the will. My initial reaction was to tell him I wanted nothing from that horrible man, but when I voiced this, he advised me not to be so hasty. He suggested I at least hear what he had to say before I made a decision.

This seemed like wise advice, so I thought for a minute before replying. "Fine, tell me whatever it is now."

"I'm afraid I can't do that. The will states you must come to us. It also states you must be alone. If you are accompanied, we are to deny you entry and throw away the letter for you."

My initial thought of asking my father to go with me vanished with this silly condition.

"Is such a thing normal?" I asked.

"We don't deal in normal wills Miss Wakefield. We only do strange requests, so I don't know how to answer that.

I will tell you, it is the first time we have come across such a condition, but on the other hand I don't find it very strange.”

“Where are your offices?” This man was English, and I wasn't going back there to hear what an old man who had refused to speak to me when he was alive, wanted to say now he was dead.

“Actually, they are in London, but for this business we have a conference room in the hotel Prince de Galles, here in Paris, that we are using as an office.”

“You keep saying we, who is we?”

“I have two partners in the firm, but I am dealing with this alone. Perhaps I misspoke and I should have said I. I am simply used to talking about my partners and myself as a ‘we’ because we run everything together.”

“I will think about it and let you know.” I needed time to come to terms with the fight that was happening inside me. Right now, the biggest part wanted nothing to do with the man, but another part was saying Philip was right, I needed to hear what he had to tell me and not dismiss it so readily.

“I'm afraid you don't have long Miss Wakefield. Another condition of the will is that you must visit us, sorry me, the same day I tell you. As the office is not really an office and I know you're busy here, I am willing to see you this evening, any time that suits.”

"I don't know. I am not going to do anything without talking to my father." Then a thought struck me. "Has my father been summonsed as well?"

"No, Miss Wakefield, just you."

"Then I definitely need to speak to my father before I can give you an answer."

"I'm sure they will let you use this phone and I will step out of the room if you would like to do it now. There isn't much time before the deadline runs out." I glanced at the clock and it was just after three in the afternoon, so he was right about time being tight. Philip looked a question at me.

I guess he was right, so I asked him to leave. I sat for some time before picking up the phone. My instinct to refuse to go was very strong, but I knew my father would be the voice of reason, so I called.

My father agreed with Philip, I needed to go to the meeting to find out what my grandfather had to say. Once I had all the information I could accept or refuse any offer made to me he pointed out. I wasn't to treat this meeting as something definitive. He also had another suggestion, and that was that I take my mobile phone with me. According to the terms laid down, I couldn't be accompanied, but it said nothing about telephoning someone for advice during the meeting. My father would stay close to the telephone that evening if I wanted to call and discuss anything with him, but he was adamant I should go. He didn't want me to regret it later on, once it was too late.

When I put the phone back down I sat thinking again, and then gathering my courage I asked Philip to come back in. I certainly was curious about what I was going to hear, and told him I would come to his hotel at eight o'clock that evening.

One friend I had made during my stay in Paris was Fabian. I trusted him so much I had told him who my grandfather was, but he was the only one who knew.
I sought him out once Philip left, and told him what was happening. Like the good friend he was, he said he would go to the hotel with me and wait in the bar. After all, the hotel was a public place, so he had the right to go for a drink in the bar without it meaning he was 'accompanying me', he pointed out. Having company on the journey there, which was a good thirty-minute drive, would be a big help, and suddenly I felt better about going.
We finished the classes that day, not that I took in much of what was said, and left immediately afterwards to go out for dinner, although I had little appetite. Fabian was his customary bubbly self, flirting with anyone who came near him, as usual.

Fabian was a contradiction in many ways; he looked like a real man's man, but was gay. At times he acted like a heterosexual male, while at others like a raving queer, and these were his words, not mine. We were the two outsiders in the group; me because I wasn't French, or from any serious wine producing country, and he because of his sexual preferences. We had formed an instant bond, and each would have done just about anything for the other.
Like me, Fabian had felt that the Comte should have been locked up, or as he suggested on more than one

occasion, sent to the guillotine. Fabian's English was excellent, and my French wasn't too bad, so we tended to converse in whatever language we felt like at the time. I wasn't sure if the lawyer spoke French are not, but if I phoned Fabian from the room, I would speak to him in French in the hope that the lawyer didn't understand. It all depended on what he wanted and why I had been summonsed, but I would only know that once I went to the appointment. That didn't stop me speculating.

Fabian had insisted on driving that evening so I could have a strong drink to set me up for the meeting. I must say, I don't think it did any good. I still felt somewhat ill as I entered the makeshift office.

Philip invited me to sit down, enquired if I wanted anything and ordered two large cognacs when I expressed that desire. Maybe the second one would do what the first hadn't; calm the butterflies in my stomach. He then opened a folder full of pages and a myriad of envelopes which looked like letters.

"I have very precise instructions about how to conduct this meeting, and I must adhere to them. Before I start, I am to give you this letter to read." He handed over a sealed envelope. I opened it and saw what my grandfather's writing was like for the first time, at least I assumed it was his.

The writing was clear and concise. It was also in English.

Georgina, you are my granddaughter. You don't know me, and I don't like you, however French law dictates I leave my estate to a member of my family, and you are my only choice, your father having refused it years before.

I leave you my wine business which I built up to be the best in the world, my Château, furnished with priceless objects, and a large amount of money in the bank. My wife and her three children are currently living in the Château, but they are to get nothing. I want that to be very clear; nothing means in any shape or form; no money, no goods, no handouts no charity, no gifts, no wages, nothing. You can do with them what you will, but you might find it useful to let them stay there. The witch runs the house very well and her three familiars, or certainly the elder two, are good at the business side of things. They will be able to help you with the enterprise. My big worry is that you will ruin everything I built up. Between them they might manage to keep things safe. I cannot force you to let them stay there. I did try, but apparently a man's home, or in your case, a girl's, is sacred, and no one can be forced on him there.

You will have a trial period of two years. You cannot sell, gift or rent the house or business during that time. You must stay there. When that period is up, a friend of mine will judge if you have made a success of my business or not. If you have, there will be another letter for you. If you haven't, it means you have ruined my business and are free to do whatever you want. Jacques, my cellar master, must stay employed for these two years. After that you and he can come to your own arrangement, whatever that might be.

If you refuse this offer, it will go to the witch and her familiars.

I am told you have an excellent pallet, which gives me some small hope for my business, but try not to run it into the ground.

You grandfather

Bert Wakefield

P.S. My son is never to set foot on any of my property.

I hadn't known what to expect, but I certainly hadn't been expecting that. I had assumed his wife would inherit everything, and all that was waiting for me was perhaps a letter apologising for his behaviour. The more I thought about it, the more something didn't seem right, so I questioned Philip.

"Can he do that? Does his wife not have a claim on all, or part of his estate?"

"I can assure you everything is legal, and the only person who could have a claim is your father. If the Countess tries to lodge a claim, I have a letter for her and a document that will stop her in her tracks, so you need have no worries there," Philip assured me.

I knew I was repeating myself, but couldn't help it. "I need to think about this." I stood up, about to say 'I will let you know', when Philip held up his hand.

"This offer disappears once you leave this room. You have to decide right now, sorry." As if wanting to help me, Philip also repeated himself. "You can use this phone if you want to make any calls. I will leave you alone," and he left the room.

I phoned my father who was just as shocked as me at the news. He was even more so when I read him the postscript on the letter.
I asked if he wished to stake his claim, and he said he was happy for me to have it.

"That means if I do accept, you cannot come to visit, and I don't like that," I said.

"Oh I can come and visit darling, don't worry. I'll buy a wheelchair and I can be wheeled around. That way we stick to the letter of the will, but I can spend some time with you."

That almost made me laugh and I had another thought, "I'll buy you a load of rugs for your room, for all the house in fact, so you can walk on those because they are my property and not the old sods. We laughed together at that idea for out-foxing someone who believed he had been so clever.

In the end Philip resolved this for us, suggesting my father contest the will and ask for half the property. That way, he could not be denied access, and if he wished he could gift his half back to me, thereby breaking the expression I objected to so strongly. Then he suddenly laughed.
"Actually, there is no problem. If you inherit it, legally it becomes your property, so you can have whoever you

wish to visit, including your father. It is no longer the Comte's property, so the clause is nothing to worry about.

As far as the inheritance was concerned, my father felt it would be foolish to refuse everything I was being offered. He pointed out I had no clear idea of what I wanted to do in two days' time once I had my certificate. Wine was a field I enjoyed in every form, and had some knowledge of, although not enough specific expertise to run a winery business. He assured me there would be people in place who knew exactly what they were doing. If I didn't like them, others could easily be found to replace them. I couldn't sell it for two years, but after that I could do what I wanted, he continued. Between the winery and the Château it would be worth a small fortune. I could open the wine shop I desired and stock it with only the best wines, if that was what I wished, he pointed out. I wouldn't even need customers as I could afford to run it any way I wanted. He laughed as he said that, although I was in such turmoil I didn't feel like joining him. The two years would pass in a flash he assured me. He went on to say that the newspapers in Britain were talking about the count's death and speculating about the multi-million pound inheritance.

I didn't know what to do and sat on the phone in silence.

My father interrupted my thoughts. "Think carefully about this question Georgina. If you inherited this from anyone else, would it interest you?"

The answer to that was simple. I found it a fascinating idea and the thought of running a winery had my heart racing with excitement. When I told my father this he said I was being silly to even think about refusing.

My mother who I knew was listening on another line joined in. "If we hadn't told you about the relationship, you would probably want it, so don't let that cloud your judgement."

"That's where you're wrong. I have come across so much information about dirty dealings and horrible tricks that my grandfather played on people, that it absolutely disgusts me. It is that, more them my relationship to him, which makes me want to refuse."

"Then, it is that, more than anything, that should make you accept the offer. You will perhaps be in a position to right some of the wrongs that were done. If you feel so strongly about them, that is a very good incentive for accepting."

As always, my father was the voice of reason. The thought of trying to repair some of the damage my grandfather had caused, did excite me.

"It isn't a good reason to refuse. The business will still exist if you don't take it, and the damage will remain done. It will change nothing for anyone, except you and whoever gets it," my father pointed out.

He had a good point. I asked him if he would come and help me, if I did accept the offer, but his reply was not the one I hoped for.

"I was about seven or eight when my father inherited the place. I was sent to boarding school in England the same year. I only ever spend brief holidays there, so I know virtually nothing about the business. I tried to avoid anything to do with my father, so did not follow him around, absorbing things when I was home. I wouldn't be of any help to you.

Also, consider how would look if the young girl who is supposed to be running the place takes her parents with her. It makes you look less business like, and less professional, at a time when you need to be strong. You will have to project the image of someone who knows exactly what they're doing. We will come to visit, and I will be available on the telephone or by email anytime you want."

I had been tempted to accept the offer, images of my father and I working together flooding my head, but that response floored me.

I sat thinking again, basically going round in circles. Philip returned, offering me another brandy and telling me to take all the time I wanted, providing he had a response before midnight, he had no problem waiting. He enquired if I wish to be left alone or not, and I replied that it didn't really matter, I was just fighting a lot of things in my head.

Philip offered to be a sounding board, and when I confessed my doubts, he agreed with my father. "If you feel so deeply about the wrongs done to other vintners, you could use your inheritance to try to repair some of the damage. That would be a wonderful thing to do."

A thought popped into my head. "Philip, it said I couldn't come accompanied by anyone, but did it mention that I couldn't have someone join me here now?"

Philip smiled, "No it didn't."

I phoned Fabian and asked him to come up.

Once he was seated and introduced, I brought Fabian up to date with everything and he instantly got extremely excited.

His first question was, "Did you get money too? Lots of money?"

"Yes."

"Great! We can open a small, boutique restaurant with a wine shop on the premises and I can run that. I will give wine tastings where I explain things to people. It'll be such fun. You don't even need to pay me until the restaurant and shop start earning money. All I need is for you to house me and feed me."

Chapter 4

"Hold on Fabian. It isn't that simple. I haven't decided if I will accept or not. Also…" He was so enthusiastic he had ignored all the problems, seeing only the fun parts.

"What? Of course you will accept. You can't possibly refuse such a wonderful opportunity," he interrupted. My friend was astonished that I didn't share his excitement.

Fabian only saw it as exciting, but even leaving aside my moral issues, there was another problem that would need sorted. "What about his wife and her children? They are living there, and from what he said in his letter, it appears they intend to continue staying there. He has left me the problem of either putting up with them or throwing them out. Either way, it will be no easy matter."

"You might like them. You can't make judgements until you have met them."

"I assume they were under the impression they would inherit everything, so they are hardly likely to be well disposed towards me when I turn up, owner of it all. It isn't a question of making judgements, it is a question of being practical. Would you like someone who had just robbed you of millions and millions? For that is how they will see it."

"Oh, I see what you mean." He thought for a very brief second, then in typical Fabian style, immediately came up with a solution. "Just throw them out. Then you will have the place to yourself and won't have a problem." He looked at the lawyer to asked if I could do that.

"Georgina can do that, but I do feel she has a valid point. They are not going to be happy that they got nothing. There is no doubt, Georgina will be in a very difficult position," the lawyer replied.

"It would also seem from my grandfather's letter, that they are currently in charge of many aspects of the business, so without their input I will have no idea of what is going on. Isn't that so?" I looked at Philip.

"It is so. The Château has over two hundred rooms, all of which the countess currently looks after very competently, but it is a very large job. Claude, her eldest son, seems to run most of the business, while Etienne her youngest son does a lot of the marketing and other similar things, I'm not quite sure what. Margo, the daughter appears to be involved with the growing of the grapes and the harvest in some way, again I'm not entirely clear about each individual role, but I do know that between them they more or less run everything. Rumours have it that they keep their staff in the dark about their affairs, so there may be no one except the family who can tell you how things are done. On the other hand, these are only rumours, therefore may not be true. I do know none of them are liked, and in many cases are feared.

"Wow! The old boy has sent you well and truly up the creek, *and* he nicked your paddle. Do you think it was deliberate? Actually, don't answer. From everything we know of him it almost certainly was, and he is probably sitting somewhere laughing to himself at the dilemma he has created for you." Finally Fabian calmed down enough to see things more clearly.

"My advice, for what it's worth, would be to go there and learn as much as you can about each aspect of the business, as quickly as you can. Then if you wish, you can replace them. That is the easiest way to stop the business suffering as far as I can see. That is obviously not legal advice, simply my opinion," Philip offered.

Yet another problem sprang to mind. "Do the family know about the will yet?"

"No, they don't. Our instructions were to give you the letter and get your answer then, one week later, we are to call the family in and discuss the will."

Philip hadn't finished. "They have already contacted us. We gave them a date for the meeting, explaining that the count had stipulated there had to be an exact waiting period before we spoke to them. They aren't happy about that, and I have had each of them on the phone threatening and insulting me every day. All that is, except Etienne, who simply enquired if there was any way to bring the date forward. He hung up without a word when I told him there wasn't."

"Doesn't sound good then," Fabian said, finally appearing to realise there was more at stake here than wine.

I had always had somewhat of a stubborn streak and the inclination to do anything I was told I shouldn't. I was sure this family didn't want me involved, but that only made me want to be involved more. My father was right, I could try and remedy some of the wrongs. Fabian was right too. If he came with me, we could end up having a lot of fun. I was now tempted to accept but needed a little more time to think carefully. I needed to be sure of my choice. It was after ten o'clock. I had over an hour yet.

I asked the two men to leave me alone with my thoughts, and sat going over what I could and should do. I needed to find someone who was an expert on running that sort of business. They would grasp everything quicker than me and would know the correct questions to ask of the family. Even though I had to keep Jacques, the current cellar master, on the payroll, another cellar master might also be a good idea, so he could keep an eye on the man my grandfather had chosen. I wanted someone not connected to my grandfather who I was sure would have my interests at heart. One thing was certain, if I did accept, I shouldn't go there before the family in residence knew about the will. Even once that happened, I would be better to leave them a cooling off period before presenting myself. Could I find the people I needed to employ in only a couple of weeks, because I couldn't really leave it any longer than that without risking the crop being returned. Who knew what the family would do to it, and that thought led me to another question.

I called Philip back in and put my idea to him. Naturally Fabian came too, but it was legal advice I needed.

"Once the family knows the harvest is not going to be theirs, if they are as bad as everyone thinks, they will probably deliberately sabotage it. How do I stop them, short of forbidding them to set foot on the land once they leave your office?"

"The count thought them capable of just that, and foreseeing such a situation, he took precautions of his own to stop that happening. I can't tell you what they are, but it just about guarantees it won't happen."

He didn't want to tell me all the details of the instructions he had at that point. The count had not forbidden him to, but still, Philip felt they were private instructions. The arrangement was that the family were to hold a press conference before the meeting with him, and the press would be given specific questions to ask before that took place. A few of these were, 'If everything is left to your brother or your sister instead of you, will you sabotage the harvest or the production process?' This was to be addressed to each family member separately. 'Can you guarantee this year's wine will be as good as ever?' Again an answer from each individual was required. 'Will you stake your good name on this year's crop being better than last year's?' each newspaper had a question they had to agree in writing to ask, before they received an invitation. That was the reason for the delay telling the family, to give the press time to reply to the invitation.

The theory was that the family were to be put in an untenable position by having them publicly declare they would be continuing as before. The count's idea was, not only to avoid sabotage, but to make them stay on when Georgina was the new boss. It might look like the reasoning behind this was to help her, but Philip, and his partners, were of the opinion that it was simply to protect the good name of the wine the nasty man had so carefully nurtured over the years. It seemed to be the only thing he cared about.
The three partners had arrived at the conclusion that all this would certainly make life easier for Georgina on the one hand, because she had experts who knew how

everything ran. However, on the other hand, it would make her life an absolute misery.
I only found all this out much later on,

I thought some more, but while I kept seeing more problems, I also kept seeing more promise. Eventually, with the clock ticking, and time running out, I accepted.

Arrangements were made. Fabian and I would graduate, each going to our own homes for a short while. We would meet back in Paris and travel to the château together about one week after the family had been informed.

Chapter 5

Things went to plan. My parents came to Paris for the ceremony before we all headed home to England.

Naturally the vineyard was the main topic of conversation the whole time I was at home. We discussed many things, with both of my parents agreeing that I should employ experts in every field I could so they could keep an eye on the family.

My mother suggested I contact everyone I had met in the wine industry and ask them if they knew of a person for each position. I really needed a large team, but to start with, the urgency was for three of four experts to learn how Château de Chivagnon wine was made. To stay at the top, the wine needed to be of a consistent quality. Once I had achieved that, I could then make some changes, if that was what I wanted. The problem was with the consistency. If the family refused to tell me how they did things, there would be differences, maybe subtle or perhaps drastic. Either way, it could ruin the reputation of Allisette in its first season under my ownership. As everyone knows, it takes years to build up a good name and only days, if not hours, to destroy it, so this was something I could not afford.

I ticked people off my list as I found suitable candidates.

I needed a winemaker. The person responsible for what was in the bottle. Eventually he would need an assistant, but time enough for that later on. Found.
Bill was Australian and had come to Europe hoping to work in a French vineyard. He had not been ready for

refusal after refusal, simply because he wasn't French, and had ended up working on a small vineyard in England, despite his excellent qualifications and experience. I liked him and felt sure he would soon become my righthand man.

A cellar master who was responsible for the wine in the barrels or tanks, whichever were used. He also did the blending to get the taste just right, as well as a host of other jobs. Jacques, the current one was the man I had to keep working there for two years, but that didn't stop me getting another. What did stop me was, I couldn't find one.

A viticulturist, basically the person in charge of all aspects of the grapes, from planting, growing and maintaining healthy grapes, to deciding, along with the winemaker, when the best time to harvest is. Found.
Fleur, of all the names possible, this one made me laugh for someone with green fingers. She was knowledgeable and a fan of both Allisette wine and the grape varieties used to make it. She would be honoured to work there. It was a dream she said, during the interview.

A general manager would also be useful, as he could oversee all aspects, including sundry items such as labels, as well as coordinating everything that happened. Found.
Lucien, a friend of Fabian's actually, who had been doing just that job for a landowner he found too demanding. The man constantly contradicted himself, leaving Lucien always doing the wrong thing. 'Put that there' was followed by 'why did you put that there?' he explained. He couldn't wait to change jobs.

Luckily my search brought forth results quickly and I had everyone I needed, except a cellar master. One of the experts, the winemaker, said he had a fair idea of what that job entailed, and I hoped that between him, Fabian and I, we could manage if we had to. I would keep looking for a cellar master though.

I explained the situation to everyone, adding that there would probably be a great deal of hostility, but none of them seemed fazed. The wine business was full of hostility they all assured me, and they had all come across their fair share of it already. I was a very rich woman now, and didn't have any money worries, so I started paying their wages immediately. Having found them, I didn't want to lose them to another winery for the sake of one month's wage.

I intended to go to the Château with Fabian and Martin and see how the land lay before getting all my workers to come over.

Discussing it with my parents, we had come to the decision to ask Philip to call the Château to inform them of my arrival. They would not be told that I was bringing anyone else with me, for I just needed to be sure that someone would be there when I arrived. The rest was not their business.

My father was the wise one in the family as far as business was concerned, but my mother was the best at personal relationship advice. She suggested I see how the family's attitude was from the very beginning and react accordingly. If they were friendly and welcoming, I should also be friendly and welcoming, while at the same time extremely wary of their motives. If, on the other hand, they were cold or even hostile, I needed to immediately make the position clear. They were guests in my home and would only stay there as long as it suited me, and I wanted them to be there.

She insisted the first impression I made was the most important and I should not let them get away with anything for the first few days. I could relax my attitude and become more lenient after that, but if I didn't put my foot down in the beginning, she was certain they would walk over me with pleasure. This, coming from a woman who was nice to everyone, had a stronger effect on me than it would have had if my father had said it.

I had hired one other person.

Martin had driven me to important meetings in the past and acted as a sort of bodyguard if I was carrying large amounts of money or valuable wine anywhere. I liked him and we often chatted. He said that he loved driving, and some clients were nice, but others were horrid, especially the women. They treated him like their own personal servant, expecting him to carry their shopping around after them, and be on call twenty-four hours a day. These same women asked specifically for Martin, and his boss insisted he drive them any time they wanted. This was more often that Martin was happy about. He actually had a degree in French, but finding teaching was not for him and other work too hard to come by, he had started as a driver for the company who provided cars for the auction house, which is how I had come to know him.

I felt sure the family living in the Château would be a threat to me in all manner of ways. Perhaps not physical, although a little research had turned up three cases of very violent aggression from Claude, each withdrawn before the court date. For that reason, I had offered Martin a large wage to come with me as a bodyguard, driver, assistant and general dogsbody. He had always liked working for me he said, and jumped at the chance. No one was to know the bodyguard part, believing only he was my assistant.

Martin and I flew to Paris, where we met up with Fabian. I had told him I wasn't sure about opening a restaurant come shop, but he insisted he wanted to work there anyway, and would be my assistant, manager, anything for free. I told him I wanted a friend, and we could see later on what role he would best suit. Naturally he was informed of my bodyguard's abilities to protect me, causing him to ask if I really felt such a precaution was necessary. As soon as I informed him of Claude's three violent attacks on people, one not very long ago, he did think perhaps it was a good idea. Luckily Martin and Fabian seemed to get on well, as that would make my life much easier.

We wanted to arrive at the Château the middle of the afternoon. This was carefully timed to avoid lunch, but leave enough time to get settled into our rooms before dinner. We left Paris in the morning, and I especially was terribly nervous. Martin had spoken to a colleague and had managed to find a wonderful large car to buy, so we were all comfortable during the journey. We stopped for lunch along the way and although I wasn't hungry, I forced myself to eat something.

As we got nearer the dreaded encounter, I started to feel sick and eventually had to ask Martin to pull over. I got out and walked around a bit. The fresh air helped, as did a few deep breaths, and I got back into the car. The two men in my life assured me I wasn't to worry, they would protect me, take care of me and backed me up in anything I wanted to say or do. I appreciate the kindness, but this didn't really help, and I still felt nauseous by the time we got to the Château.

Over the car pulled up, so the Countess appeared. I knew she wasn't really a Countess, for my grandfather hadn't been a count, but my mother suggested I address her by the title she had chosen to use, rather than call her by her name, Esme, as that might help get her more on my side.

Her first words made my nausea vanish instantly.

"Welcome to my home." I felt Fabian's hand on my arm, which I assume was destined to stop me saying, 'this is not *your* home'.

"Hello," I said, avoiding both her title and her name. I had no desire to honour this woman by calling a Countess, but I also knew it wasn't wise to antagonise her too much by using her Christian name, at least not yet.
The first night Fabian, Martin and I walked into the house, I had to be strong. The two men at my side helped give me that strength. My own family had stated how important it was to show this family, who were actual residents, who was boss, and prove it was no longer them.

For that reason, once we were inside, when the Countess said in a very cold tone, "I have had the pink room prepared for you," I replied, "Thank you. I will look at them all and decide which one I want." Without waiting for an answer I headed towards the stairs.

"You can't do that. We are using some of them and they are private. How dare you even suggest you look in our rooms." This was delivered in a biting tone, designed to show me she was the boss and I an unwelcome intruder.

"No one told me there would be more than one person, I will now have to get the staff to prepare more rooms, and I don't know if there is time." She wasn't going to give up.

"Madame, I believe you are under the mistaken impression that this is still your house. It isn't. I will choose where I wish to sleep, and I will sleep in that room. There is nothing you can do about that except leave. Now, as I said, I will look at all the rooms, then decide. Once my friends have chosen their rooms you will have them prepared immediately. You will make time. Is that clear?" I walked upstairs without waiting for an answer, and heard Fabian whisper behind me, "She is stabbing you in the back with her eyes." I had no doubt that was the case, but I also had no doubt I had firmly established the pecking order in the house. I just hoped it lasted.

As it turned out the pink room was exactly what it sounded like, a pink room, far too much so for my tastes. I didn't want the room she was in because it was the one my grandfather had used, but of the remaining rooms I like the yellow room best and no one was in it. Fabian liked the Rose room, which currently the daughter was in, and Martin had no preference, providing his room was close to mine he said. That left him the blue room, also unoccupied.
Fabian offered to take the green room, but I told him I would get the daughter to move. He said he would prefer

not. He thought it was too early on to make that sort of enemy of her, as well as her mother, and he would be fine in the green room, for now.

We went downstairs and with difficulty, by opening every door in the hall, we found a family sitting together in a room. They were obviously discussing us because all talk stopped when we walked in.

"Good afternoon, I am Georgina," I said to the room in general. "Comtesse de Chivagnon, we have decided which rooms we wish to use. Would you care to ask the staff to prepare them, or shall I do it?" I thought I would throw her this bone, but in the end I needn't have bothered.

"Do it yourself." She had looked at me like dirt and immediately looked away again. I wasn't going to have this.

"Esme, I have already told you, you…"

"My name is Comtesse de Chivagnon. Please have the courtesy to use my title."

"Really? Are we going to do this? You are not a countess. My grandfather was not a count. You use a made-up title, it isn't real. As for courtesy, this is my house, you are a guest and that demands certain courtesies towards me, your host. Now, once again, this is my house. You only have the right to stay here as long as I wish it. One more word, look or expression from you like the ones you have given me already, and you will be leaving immediately. Is that clear?"

She didn't look at me, nor did she answer.

"I will ask you again for the last time, is that clear?"

"Yes," she almost spat.

"Get the yellow room, the blue room and the green room prepared immediately. I did not say please because I intend to treat you exactly the way you treat me. If you don't like it then try treating me better and you will get better treatment, if you stay that is."

I introduced my two friends, (for Martin was fast becoming a friend as well as employee), to the three children. I got a lot of hostility from the elder two, and indifference for Etienne. This was exactly what Philip had said. The youngest didn't seem as bad as the others, but it wasn't something I felt I could count on until I knew him better.

The siblings simply said hello and told me their names, nothing more, nothing less.

"We would like some tea or coffee after our journey, with biscuits or cake. Which of you will organise that for us?" There were no volunteers as Esme stood up and muttered that she was going to organise the rooms. As she left the room she added that she would get something sent in.

Martin, Fabian and I sat down while I made a little speech I had practiced on my friends earlier.

"I am well aware that you don't want me here, but here I am. Now, we can either work together or you can leave.

The choice is yours. One thing I would say, make sure it is your choice and not mine. If I encounter hostility, intolerance, obstinance or any negative behaviour, you will have five minutes to leave the property. I have the legal right and believe me I will do it."

No one said anything, they just looked daggers at me.

Claude broke the silence. "What makes you think you have a right to come here?"

"I don't think I have the right, I do have the right Bert was my grandfather. He is no relation to you, and no relation to your mother."

That little gem had come from Philip. It was the ace in the hole that my grandfather had used to stop his wife inheriting anything. When they were married, he was married as the Comte de Chivagnon, a man he was not. That meant there actually was no marriage, so his wife wasn't his wife.

"You don't have to like the situation, but you will only stay here if one condition is met. I must either like you or find you pleasant enough to be around. I have my own expert winemakers, vintners etcetera arriving soon, so contrary to what you may think, I don't need you. If you make an effort to be pleasant, and that does not mean we have to become friends, it means you will be polite and respectful, then I will let you stay. The first time you go too far you're gone. That includes your mother, so perhaps if she wishes to stay, you need to speak to her. She has already pushed me further than I want to go. The only thing that has saved her so far is because I have just arrived and you don't know me. You don't know that if I say I will do something, then I will do it."

Fabian jumped in at this point, "I know her very well and I can guarantee she will do what she says." Martin added his voice to that affirmation too.

I wasn't sure if it if I should say more or ask questions, but I was saved having to make a choice by coffee and cake arriving.

Margot reached towards the coffee pot to pour it and then seemed to think better of it. "I assume you would all like coffee?" She queried.

We said we would, and as it had been put in front of her, I couldn't fault her for choosing to pour out for everyone. She asked Etienne to pass round the cups and the cake. Her mother hadn't returned by the time we had finished. I assumed she was huffing or fuming somewhere. Did I leave her alone, or did I send for her. Perhaps she was in my room cutting up all my clothes. I suddenly had a vision of a mad woman with a pair of scissors, but thought it was ridiculous. I didn't really think she would stoop so low, although you never know.

"Perhaps one of you could see what is keeping your mother and find out if our rooms are ready, if you wouldn't mind," I said in as mild a tone as I could manage. Etienne jumped up, offering to go. He returned with his mother about five minutes later.

"Ms Wakefield," she emphasised the Ms, making it sound like it had five or six 's'es and Wakefield was a dirty word, "your rooms are ready."

"I would prefer it if you called me Georgina," I said. I hated 'Ms' for it sounded like a diehard feminist. I also disliked 'Miss' because it sounded like a spinster, which is why I preferred people simply to use my name. She said nothing.

Fabian, Martin and I stood up, "Are our bags already in our rooms?" Fabian asked.

"Naturally."

"Thank you."

We left the room without another word being exchanged.

Chapter 6

When we got to my room, we all went in and closed the door. Deep sighs of relief came from all of us. "That was really rotten," Fabian stated. "I mean really, really rotten."

"Now do you see what I mean?" I asked him

"I hadn't thought it would be that bad. I'm glad you brought Martin, you might need him."

Martin too had something to say, "I think you might be right about Claude. I don't like the look of him. I've seen that expression on many bad guys and nothing good ever came after of them or anyone near them. We need to be careful."

That was one thing I hadn't wanted to be right about, but at least I had had the foresight to get some sort of protection against this family.

I realised we hadn't asked about dinner, therefore had no idea what time it happened, where or whether these people dressed up for it or not. The strange thing was, we had seen no staff yet and that was another hurdle I was going to have to face.

I suggested we all unpack and meet again in the hall in about half an hour. I wanted backup with me when I faced everyone.

The rooms were very sumptuous, if a bit over-the-top, but I didn't really take anything in. There was too much unpleasantness going on, with more to come, for me to appreciate any sort of beauty in furnishings.

When we met in the hall we went first to the room we had had coffee in, but it was empty. We couldn't find anyone anywhere, leading us all to wonder if this was deliberate. We split up, wandering around the house, opening doors and looking in rooms until eventually we found the kitchen where two ladies were busy making food. I greeted them, and after telling them my name, explained I was the new owner. I asked one of them if there was a head of staff. When she informed me there was a butler who was in charge, I asked her to get him. She hesitated. Was I going to have to do this again with the staff I wondered. "Now, if you don't mind." My tone left no doubt that she was to obey, and she did.

It wasn't long before the butler came. I greeted him, introduced myself, explained the situation and asked him to gather all the staff in the kitchen.

"We normally have meetings in the hall madam," he informed me.

"We are having this meeting in the kitchen." I was watching carefully, but there was very little hesitation before he said, "Yes madam," and left. I wasn't sure if he was too well trained, or if he had accepted me as the new boss.

It was actually a smaller staff than I would have imagined for such a large house. I went through the whole thing of explaining my position and telling them my name again. Then I said, "As the château is now mine, you all work for me. I would like you to remember that. You have been taking orders from," and here I hesitated for they are knew her as the Countess. Did I ruin her credibility by telling them the truth or did I give her one last chance? "The Countess, so you may not be happy to change that. If any of you wish to leave I would like to know now, otherwise your orders come from me. If they do not come from me, Fabian, indicating my friend, or Martin, indicating Martin, then you do not follow them, no matter what they are, or who gives them. Is that clear?"

There were a few muttered yeses, but nothing the left me feeling confident about the situation.

"Do any of you wish to leave?" No one moved

"Have any of you any questions?"

"What about the Countess? This is her home." Someone, I think the head housekeeper asked.

I thought quickly and made a decision. "First, the Countess is not a Countess. She pretends to be nobility, but she has no title. Second, she was not married to my grandfather, so this house is not and never was hers. Third they haven't been together very long. This house originally belonged to my grandmother a real Countess, not my grandfather, before the lady you call Countess arrived here. It has been in my family for a considerable time."

There were a lot of startled looks, but there were also some disbelieving ones, and I foresaw trouble with those people.

I left everyone in silence for a while, hoping someone would speak up. I could see they had much to complain about but didn't want to do it to my face. I didn't want them doing it behind my back.

"What am I to do when the Countess gives me an order. I can't refuse her." The same lady queried.

"That's not a problem. If you feel unable to refuse her, you can leave." I realised that sounded more like I was offering her a choice. "When I said, 'you can leave', what I really meant is; you will leave. You are fired. I do not intend to live in a house where I need to watch my back and the people are not prepared to follow my requests. I am a very reasonable person. People who have worked with me in the past have enjoyed the experience, but I will not tolerate a lack of respect for my orders, even if they are couched in the form of a request or question.

They were all shocked. "If she goes, I go," said another lady.

"Goodbye." I then added as they both still sat there, "what are you doing still here? Leave now. Martin would you mind helping them find the door please?"

"It will be an absolute pleasure," he said.

Now I will try once more. "Do any of you wish to leave?" There was no reply. Fabian said to me in a voice meant to be heard, "Looks like we'll be going to a restaurant for dinner if they don't answer and you sack them all."

The Inheritance Mysteries, Wine and Lies continues

If you enjoyed this, continue the mysterious inheritance in books 2, 3 and 4

There are many twists and turns to come for Georgina. Her inheritance will be anything but plain sailing.

She still has some serous battles with the Countess, Claude and Margot to come, although Etienne, appears to be trustworthy and interested only in making good wine. She is unsure if he really is all he seems or not, and watches him to find out.

Then there is a part of her inheritance which is illegal, and when she discovers this, something needs to be done. What to do is the problem, as this provides the majority of the income for the business.

As she attempts to right some of the wrongs her grandfather did, she finds a way to help another vintner, while making more wine for her own winery. The problem is the man has lost even the will to live. Never mind the drive to make wine.

Two years after her grandfather dies another letter from him awaits her. This one is horrible and contains many secrets. Some to her advantage, others so bad she struggles to carry on after reading it.

The Inheritance Mysteries

Already published in the Inheritance Mystery Series;

The Inheritance Mysteries, A Mysterious Box

'The Mysterious Box' series follows Gillian's seemingly simple inheritance of a book shop and house, but then things are not always what they seem. A discovery in a box in the storeroom of her new shop leads Gillian on a journey to either death or riches. Her life changes drastically in other ways too as she moves to her new house. New friendships and old ones, lead to all sorts of complications and delights along the way.

The Inheritance Mysteries, An Old Partnership

This series is about two men who, many years ago, at the beginning of the gold rush, opened a gold mine together. Their road to riches was neither long nor tortuous, but life for their sons was. As the gold started to run out their lives had to change drastically, and it is the repercussions of these changes that made their inheritance odd, to say the least. There is a very strange bet with a cowboy, a native Indian cousin and a scheming mother.

Coming Soon in the Inheritance Mystery Series;

The Inheritance Mysteries, To Do List

What happens when an odious and controlling father hates Mungo, his son, but has no one else to leave his vast inheritance to?
Why a long list of things the son has to do in order to inherit, of course. However, nothing is quite what it seems, and even a simple month-long cruise could end up becoming the rest of his life in a totally unexpected way.

What is the point of Mungo spending time working in a vineyard, or travelling across continents on a train?
The answer will only be revealed once Mungo has completed every seemingly pointless task on the list.

When he has finished, there are two inheritances. Depending on some mysterious factor, he will inherit one or other, both or neither of these.